The Cuckoo Pit
and
Little Jenny Wren

Jo Brodie

Copyright © 2018 Jo Brodie

Cover illustration © 2018 Jo Brodie

All rights reserved.

ISBN:1985402122
ISBN-13:9781985402126

This is a work of fiction. Names, characters, places, and incidents either are the products of the author's imagination or are used fictitiously. Any resemblance to actual persons, living or dead, businesses, companies, events, or locales is entirely coincidental.

CONTENTS

	Acknowledgments	i
1	The Cuckoo Pit	1
2	Little Jenny Wren	20

ACKNOWLEDGMENTS

I would like to give a big 'thank you' to George Nicholson and Susan Condor, who read and edited both stories and suggested subtle changes to improve them.

To Tracy Cook, who works tirelessly for the benefit of Greyhound welfare and the rescue group GRACE based in the north east of the U.K.

For my own Little Jenny Wren.

THE CUCKOO PIT

Mrs Pinkerton bustled into the drawing room of her elegant manor house, and checked the windows for any smudges left by the maid, who, she felt sure, would leave a fingermark if not corrected sharply.

She looked past the shutters as her neighbours trotted past the immaculate front garden, with its regiment of colourful flowers marching across the borders edging the lawn. They were kept that way by the recently employed gardener. Mrs Pinkerton liked everything kept in its place, and that included the perennials.

Her small lips pursed together and her nose twitched as she watched the two ladies glance at the manor house, then turn to each other, whispering behind their hands. Gossiping no doubt, she thought with disapproval, a frown settling over her rather long pointed features.

She trotted away, constantly checking with busy hands that everything was in its correct place The cushions were puffed up and artfully piled onto the stylish but uncomfortable sofa, in a pleasing parade of tapestry designs. Wow betide that anyone should be rude enough to actually sit on them!

She moved a small ornament on the fireplace mantle an inch to the right. It had to be just so. She adored her grand country house with its stately Georgian windows and wonderful roomy dimensions and had furnished it with some style and a substantial amount of money.

She had longed to raise herself above the life of her parents, although they had worked hard and now lived comfortably, and she set herself the goal of marrying well. After meeting Mr Pinkerton at a social gathering she decided he was the one and walked him up the aisle as quickly as he could be induced to move his thin frame.

She then obligingly produced three children over the years and encouraged her husband to further his career at every opportunity. The twin girls she had insisted on naming India and China to make them sound as exotic and mysterious as possible. As they grew into moody, sullen teenagers it became as plain as the noses on their faces that their names were the only exotic thing about them.

It was when the boy arrived that Mr Pinkerton put his foot down and refused to call him Caesar, settling for Henry, a good, solid name. It was possibly the only thing Mr Pinkerton had ever been difficult about.

Her husband was as tall and thin as she was small and rotund. A shrewd investor, he had done surprisingly well for himself and his family, and then very neatly passed away with barely a murmur. He left sufficient funds for the grieving widow to buy the country manor house, employ a maid, cook and gardener, and to be regarded with some envy by her village acquaintances.

Mrs Pinkerton made her way to the kitchen, nodded to the cook and began looking through the cupboards, mentally listing the ingredients required for the dinner party she was presenting the following evening.

Tapping across the floor she wrote down a long and detailed list of food, spices, herbs, puddings and then listed flowers to decorate the dinning table. Raising her pointed nose she said to the cook, 'There is the menu, and mind that the ingredients are all fresh! I want the best for my guests.'

The cook sketched a curtsey. 'Yes, ma'am.' As Mrs Pinkerton bustled away she picked up the list and read through it.

There was enough to feed a family of four for a month. Sighing, she laid aside her apron and picked up her coat. How she was supposed to find fresh salmon, quails eggs and blueberries and raspberries in a small country village twenty miles from the nearest town she didn't know. The only option was a trip further afield. The one consolation was that it got her out of Mrs Pinkerton's way for a while.

Mrs Pinkerton had recently attended the Rectory summer fete, and had met Mr Porke, a man who she felt had all the attributes for a future husband. He was a big, expansive man, rather on the heavy side, with a booming voice and a hearty laugh, and a habit of rocking back on his heels and patting his stomach when he made a witticism. Mrs Pinkerton had liked what she had seen.

A few discreet enquiries had revealed he was a widower. So many of us she thought with a sigh, and that he had a hefty fortune made from farming pigs and producing 'The Original Porke Sausage!' swiftly followed by the phenomenally successful 'The Original Porke Pie!' He had a young son who was in his last years at school, and a very large bank balance all of which made him suitable spouse material.

She had invited him to her dinner party, and she was proud of the sumptuous meal in the making. She was determined to charm and woo him. She did not mind an extra child in the house. A sweet stepson would fit in very nicely. She would be the envy of all her acquaintances, and finances would never become a problem.

Thinking of these things Mrs Pinkerton also vowed when married to keep her name along with his. There was nothing so upper class as a double barreled name, and Mrs Pinkerton-Porke had a noble ring to it. Her nose twitched again, and she smiled to herself with her imaginings as she nibbled at her luncheon sandwiches, prepared in advance for her by the cook.

She thought of the dress laid out upstairs with discreet but expensive jewelry to compliment it and a satisfied expression crossed her face.

* * *

Mr Porke was dressing for the dinner. A large man, he had recently seen a tailor in London and was admiring the cut of his expensive suit in the mirror. His home, though not as magnificent as Mrs Pinkerton's, did him and the boy nicely.

His son, Percival, sat on the edge of his father's bed, watching as his father preened himself and patted at the expensive jacket. Mr Porke turned and looked at the boy, surrounded by his school books, and wondered again how he and the late Mrs Porke had managed to produce such a beautiful angelic child.

The late Mrs Porke had been his childhood sweetheart. Although she was no beauty, she had been devoted to his care, loyal, and immensely practical and they had rubbed along nicely.

She had expired shortly after the arrival of the angel child leaving him to arrange a nursery maid and an aupair as time progressed. Now, with the boy just in his last years of schooling he had dispensed with these services as he had set his sights on a widow, recently met.

As ever, Mr Porke studied the boy with bewildered but proud eyes. How he had sired such beauty, he did not know. A crown of blond silk hair, large, pale blue eyes with the longest eyelashes he had ever seen, a slightly aquiline nose and a firm masculine mouth and chin sat upon a long-limbed elegant adolescent frame, and the sweetest disposition he could ever have wished for.

'Well, lad, I'm off to see the widow Pinkerton tonight,' he said gruffly. 'I am hoping she will be interested in a merger between us. We have been too long without a wife and mother in the house. Not that she could ever take the place of your sainted mother, but I need a partner my boy.'

The beautiful boy smiled, revealing neat white teeth. 'I hope you have a good evening, father.'

'Right. Well, I am off now, mind you do your homework, lad. Good grades will stand you in good stead for the rest of your life.' He awkwardly patted his son's head, smoothed down his jacket lapel, collected his hat from the hat stand and left, whistling cheerfully.

The angel child climbed from the bed, stretching and yawning like a sleek cat, and switched the curtain back to watch his father striding up the street. Yes, definitely gone, he thought, and then pulled from his pocket a handful of change and small notes that he had stolen from his father's coat pocket earlier.

He counted it out. Enough for fish and chips and a film at the local cinema. The girl on the ticket office was sweet on him and sometimes let him in for free. Percival glanced at his homework and then packed the books up and took them to his room.

There was no need to do any homework. That snotty cry baby that he had beaten up earlier at school would do it for him in the morning before his lessons. He slipped on his boots and coat, and then like his dad, strode off with a loose long limbed stride that made the girls stare as he passed by.

Mrs Pinkerton's dinner party was a huge success. Her guests oohed and aahed over the selection of courses and the quality and quantity of offerings presented to them. There was the tinkering of glasses filled with champagne, laughter and cultured conversation, which at times Mrs Pinkerton was shocked to think bordered on gossip.

As the meal progressed she had Mr Porke literally eating out of her hand, tempting him with exotic delicacies presented on delicate silver cutlery. She had simpered and flirted and he had responded in a very masculine way, to her delight. He held her hand tightly, looked into her small, beady eyes and professed his love for her when they were alone on the terraced south side of the garden under the starlit sky. It was a beautiful setting and fulfilled any romantic dreams Mrs Pinkerton might have had in her prosaic body.

It seemed that they both had the same agenda, and Mrs Pinkerton was delighted with the results.

Mr Porke continued to court her in the old fashioned way, much to her enjoyment and the entertainment of local gentry. A few weeks later she was happy to accept his marriage proposal, on his bended knee, with certain caveats. These were for them to remain together in the manor house rather than moving into his less grandiose home, and the addition of the double-barreled name she desperately wanted.

Mr Porke was happy to indulge his fiancée and merely smiled indulgently. 'As you wish, my dear.'

Mrs Pinkerton was introduced to Percival at a later meeting. She was completely bowled over by the charming boy, so fair of face, so handsome and so attentive. Much as she disliked the name Percival she disliked the shortened Percy even more and strangely, the name seemed to suit him. I will always call him Percival, she thought to herself, it's not his fault his mother did not have the wit to christen him with a better name.

Her own children, who seemed to take an irrational dislike to the golden boy, suddenly looked heavy and lacking in grace. The girls were even more boot-faced in his presence, and young Henry began stammering nervously when Percival cast his splendid limpid gaze upon him. Mrs Pinkerton could only assume it was jealousy.

However, they seemed to like Mr Porke, who was friendly and chatty with them, so Mrs Pinkerton settled down to plan a sumptuous wedding. Such a shame she had to dismiss the maid, for who else would have stolen that delightful silver salver displayed in the elegant front room?

A new maid arrived in time for the wedding. She was an older woman with gimlet eyes that seemed permanently trained on Percival.

Mrs Pinkerton was a little shocked at that level of attention to her new soon-to-be stepson, who lounged in the chairs and in the salon reading his homework books. He was so stunning that she had to admit to covert glances herself at times, and merely frowned darkly when she caught her maid's obsessive gaze remaining on the boy slightly too long.

The wedding day itself was everything that Mrs Pinkerton could have wished for.

Her children and Percival formed the train of bridesmaids and male attendants to sweep in the wake of her dazzling wedding dress trail, and Mr Porke looked magnificent in his bridal suit. The ring itself featured tiny pigs running in a circle with a heart and diamonds in the middle. Mrs Pinkerton-Porke's bosom swelled with rapture as singing filled the little country church to its rafters.

Once the wedding party returned to the house, they were greeted with champagne flutes, and canapés, and everything that could be was extravagant, opulent and lavish in every detail. Every flounce and ribbon embellished, every flower posy double in size, exotic and rare foods set upon the table. The ceilings festooned with nets and lights glittered and sparkled and tiny mirrors set within the nets reflected the candlelit tables.

There was feasting and drinking, and dancing in the ornate manor house gardens The aristocracy that she had invited nodded their heads to her and Mrs Pinkerton-Porke knew that she had finally broken through to acceptance in those higher circles. Never mind the money it had cost to get them to the wedding, she decided. It had been worth it.

Percival enjoyed the wedding. He was impressed with the manor house, and he had already hooked his stepmother into his web, as she was obviously keen to draw him into the bosom of her family.

The twins looked down their long noses at him and he had no desire to get to know them in any way. India and China had made it plain to him that his usual charm failed miserably on them. He had the uncomfortable feeling that they saw straight through him, along with that new maid who had seen him pinching money from his father's wallet.

Henry he wrote off as a stammering idiot who he would be able to manipulate easily. Perhaps due to not having a mother, he had already decided that he wanted everything for himself, and the other children in the house would have to become second place in his new mother's affections.

Percival smiled to himself. He knew how to be as charming and pleasing as possible, and as he had always been extremely spoilt by his father, he had no doubts that he would soon be the cherished son. With his handsome, boyish charm, angelic looks and unfailing courteous manners, he knew how to impress. He spent hours studying himself in the mirror, deciding which expression suited him better, practicing his smile and learning how to flick his hair back with an ease which looked completely natural and unaffected.

India and China disliked Percival with a passion. Jealous of his amazing good looks, they studied him with dark, watchful eyes, and soon found him wanting. His angelic demeanor hid a will of steel and a selfishness that would have got their ears boxed had they shown this in their character to their mother. They found him sly, devious and narcissistic with the ability to lie so convincingly that at times they doubted their own eyes.

It seemed at every turn since their mother's remarriage their belongings were rifled through, their friends beguiled away by the golden boy, and every accident or mishap was placed at their door. Their mother became harshly critical of them, complaining of their clumsiness, accusing them of upsetting the cook by stealing from the pantry, and of neglecting their schooling.

Percival smirked at the door as he listened and then disappeared into the wood to finish burning the twin's school text books and their hours of laborious notes.

India and China whispered plans together in their bedroom. They had no intention of putting up with Percival, and had formulated several strategies before they hit on the idea of writing a long letter to their aunt in London. In it they asked if they could visit for the summer as they had finished their exams early and they wanted their mother and Mr Pinkerton-Porke to have time together as newly-weds.

They hoped to appeal to their auntie's romantic nature, and if she agreed, they had no intention of returning home again. Their auntie had a lovely big house in a fashionable part of London, and the girls were keen to leave the irritating and ingratiating Percival behind. With their two heads together, they had hatched a plan to escape from the manor house and the hideous step brother.

Blaming Percival was unlikely to achieve anything other than to bring down their mother's wrath upon their heads as they had discovered to their cost.

So when the letter arrived at the breakfast table with their invitation to stay in London for the summer, the girls were elated and could barely suppress their glee. Mr Pinkerton-Porke pored over the letter with some surprise, and his wife with delight.

Two teenage girls who were turning into surly and difficult teenagers and who were constantly blaming their adorable step-brother for their failings had been difficult to deal with. Mrs Pinkerton-Porke clapped her hands together.

'India, China! Come quickly girls! You are off to see Aunt Valetta for the summer so we have to pack and get you both ready! Come along girls, come along!'

Several hours later they were ready and waiting at the door. Each twin clutched a suitcase in one hand and a small bag in the other. Mr Pinkerton-Porke drew up to the front door in his magnificent Bentley. He opened the doors of the car and swept them a bow with a hearty smile.

'Your carriage awaits miladies!' and he laughed loudly, 'off to London we go!' and giggling, the girls stepped forward.

Suddenly Percival ran forward and placed a kiss on each of the twin's cheeks. 'I will miss you, sisters.' He said, and stood wringing his hands together.

Mrs Pinkerton-Porke's heart melted. Such a sweet boy. She grasped her stepson's hand tightly in hers, and her silent son Henry's hand in the other. Raising both their clutching hands they all waved the girls goodbye.

Toot! Toot! Went the Bentley's horn. Inside the car both girls looked at each other and carefully wiped their cheeks free of Percival's kiss and dropped their hankies out of the window. Giggling again they began to regale Mr Pinkerton-Porke with stories about their aunt Valetta, and his loud guffaw could be heard as the car vanished into the distance.

Mrs Pinkerton-Porke disappeared upstairs to tidy the girls rooms which were covered in discarded clothes.

'I will miss you,' repeated Percival softly. 'NOT.' He caught Henry staring at him. 'What are you staring at?'

'N-n-n-nothing' stammered Henry. Percival frightened him. Henry had been in awe of the angel child when he had first arrived, but petty cruelties, spitefulness and lying and blaming others had soon cleared the film from his eyes. With the twins gone, any protective cloak was also removed, and he felt vulnerable and scared.

'K-k-k-keep it that way.' Mimicked Percival. 'And stay out of my way.'

Later that day Mrs Pinkerton-Porke took both boys out for a treat, and Percival was happy to upstage the silent Henry all day. In the evening, when he lay in his bed, his smile turned to a frown.

The girls had gone and he shuddered with relief that he didn't have to look at their long, thin faces and listen to their shrill voices anymore.

That left only Henry, who was still clinging to his mother, and would be more difficult to dislodge. He would need to work out a plan of action. He nibbled his fingernails thoughtfully before slipping into sleep.

Percival had teamed up with the local school bullies, gradually becoming the leader of a small group who extorted pocket money or school lunch money from their victims. He beat up the brainier, geeky children and in return for leaving them alone had all his homework done for him.

So Percival began the slow and systematic bullying of Henry. He bullied the smaller boy at school, threatened the boy's friends into leaving Henry isolated and alone. Percival even returned home sporting a shiny black eye that he tearfully told a shocked Mr and Mrs Pinkerton-Porke 'Henry did it.'

It appeared that whenever anything went wrong Henry was at the bottom of it. Mrs Pinkerton-Porke began to lose patience with her boy. Fighting at school was almost unforgivable, although her husband seemed less worried. 'Boys will be boys,' he said and patted his wife's arm.

There were incidents in the house where money disappeared, lovely, expensive ornaments were broken, and cakes were stolen from the pantry. Mrs Pinkerton-Porke found the missing money, she told her husband darkly, in Henry's room, although a tearful Henry denied taking it.

Mr and Mrs Pinkerton-Porke conferred, and decided to take Henry to a counsellor for help with his problems.

Percival was outraged. His plan was not going to schedule. He didn't want his parents spending time with that little brat and giving him extra outings and attention. He needed some fresh ideas.

One day, idly walking back from school with his mates, they told him about the old mine just off the footpath they walked down every day. The mine entrance was hidden in the long grass of the bank, and the old workings were overgrown with a wooded copse, ferns and brambles.

'Show me.' He demanded, and the lads led him to the entrance, half covered in stones, barbed wire and some wooden boarding.

One of the boys said, 'They say its a fair drop down in there. It goes down pretty deep.'

Percival peered closer and began to pull the wooden boards away from the entrance. 'Come on, lets go and look.'

For once there was silence behind him, and he looked back to see the small group of boys shaking their heads and backing away. 'No mate,' one of them muttered. ' Me dad would murder me.'

No blandishment would move them, and Percival had to concede to their joint will. He walked with them, his burnished head at an angle as he pretended to listen to their silly stories, but his mind was elsewhere.

It had looked damp and dismal in that mine shaft. Percival began to smile as a plan formed in his mind and he surprised his mates by slapping their shoulders and suggesting a game of football. Eager to get rid of some energy the small group of boys set off to the local rec and set up goalposts of clothing and set to the serious business of scoring goals.

One sunny afternoon Percival fell into step beside Henry who was hurrying home from school along the track. A quick glance up and down the track from Percival to see that they were alone, and then he grabbed Henry by the elbow and dragged him up the bank towards the mine shaft.

'What's the matter!' cried the frightened boy, 'I did your homework for you!'

Percival smiled sunnily at Henry. 'Well done. I just want to show you something. Come on.'

Henry followed warily. He rubbed his bruised elbow, and reluctantly followed as Percival scrambled up the bank. Percival was busy pulling some wood away from a large hole. Henry came closer and Percival turned his golden head, large blue eyes smiling at Henry.

'Take a look in there Henry, see if you can see what I saw.'

Henry knelt hesitantly at the edge. 'What am I looking for?' he asked, and then let out a scream as Percival forced him forward, and dropped him into the hole.

He fell into the darkness, crying and screaming Percival's name.

'What are you looking for?' shouted Percival down the hole into the darkness. 'Try looking for the way out!' And with that he forced the wooden planks back into place, replaced the stones and clambered back down the bank. He washed his hands in the little stream by the footpath and waited for a few minutes. If he couldn't hear Henry's cries then neither would anyone else. Satisfied, he thrust his hands in his pockets and whistled his way home.

Henry winded and in darkness, sobbed in terror, calling Percival's name over and over. His shins were bruised from the fall and he had dirt and dust in his hair. Struggling to his feet, he tried to claw his way back up to the entrance but the gradient defeated him and he fell back time after time. Sobbing with dread, feeling the oppressive weight of the rock all around him, he finally fell to the floor exhausted and frozen from the wet that dripped through the rocks onto him.

He lay curled up and shaking for some time, until raising his head he saw a light appear, glowing in the distance, further along the pit shaft. Wiping the sweat, tears and dirt from his face, and feeling his way along the wet rock, he made his way towards it.

That night Henry did not return from school. As the evening wore on, Mr and Mrs Pinkerton-Porke became more and more concerned. They tried speaking to Henry's friends, but no one had seen him after he left school. Percival shook his glossy head and smiled sadly into his stepmother's face.

No, he hadn't seen Henry either, he said, but he knew Henry had friends who were 'a bad lot' and that he had often bunked off school with these lads.

Mrs Pinkerton-Porke called the police.

The inspector arrived with his notebook and interviewed them all. Then the search began, the police dogs arrived, police swarmed up and down knocking on doors, and questioning neighbours.

Percival was enthralled and appalled for the same reason. He loved the fuss and drama surrounding the search, and was equally astounded that it was all for HENRY.

He had not realised how exciting it would be to see the dogs running down the street, and the weeping and wailing of his stepmother. Even his father looked tired and strained.

He suddenly wished that he had thought of hiding and being searched for, instead of Henry. He would have ensured that he was reunited after a few hours away and restored to the bosom of his new family and all this excitement and turmoil would have been for him.

Henry was gone all that night and part of the next day.

Mrs Pinkerton-Porke's face was blotched with tears, and she clung to her husband's broad arm. Percival watched jealously as neighbours arrived to offer support and sympathy. There was even a visit from Sir Smeaton-Smogg and his lady wife.

And then suddenly the police returned, screaming up the drive in their cars with the sirens going, coming to a sliding stop outside the main door of the manor. The doors were flung open and out spilled the detective on the case who turned to lead out a disheveled, dirty and tired Henry. Mrs Pinkerton-Porke ran forward with a scream and clutched him to her ample bosom, covering him in kisses and sobbing into his hair, regardless of the mess and dirt that clung to him.

The inspector firmly set her aside and led the way into the drawing room and indicated that the parents and Henry were to follow him. He turned and shut the door in Percival's angelic face. Fuming and uneasy as to what Henry was about to reveal, Percival hung about, listening at the keyhole. The story he heard was remarkable and made his fists clench with anger and jealousy.

Although upset, bedraggled, and worse for wear, Henry seemed remarkably unscathed. With the policeman taking notes and asking questions Henry clutched his mother's hand and began to explain what had happened to him.

He had been walking home and had somehow strayed off the path and fallen down the old mine shaft partially concealed on the bank by the woods. Henry was scared enough of Percival to know what would happen if he told the truth. He had enough wit about him to know that there was no point in placing blame on the angelic monster that he knew would be hiding and listening behind the door.

Henry told the policeman that he had fallen some twenty feet and had been winded and shocked when he landed at the bottom. He had seen light further along the tunnel and made his way cautiously along the mine shaft.

Once there he appeared to be in some sort of cavern space within the old mine workings. He could see quite clearly as lanterns flickered all around the area, notches in the walls were filled with lit candles and a small stream ran through one side of the cave.

The policeman's pen paused, then he went on writing as the boy continued. He had looked around for some sort of exit, and found that the walls of each tunnel were well lit, and embedded with jewels of topaz, diamonds, rubies and sapphires, sparkling and glowing in the light from the candles.

The adults in the room looked at each other. The policeman tapped his pen on the table, slowly turned over another page in his note pad and said kindly, 'Well my lad, that's quite a story! You'd best tell it all.'

So Henry told of finding a stone table laden with cut sandwiches, and his favourite dinner of pie and mash which he had devoured hungrily. There was pop on the table, and once he had satisfied his thirst and hunger he had grown sleepy and must have dozed through the night. When he awoke a little yellow canary perched on the edge of the table singing cheerfully. It had swooped around his head and then flown down one of the tunnels and he had leapt to his feet and followed it. It had led him to an exit high in the woods where he had managed to crawl out and make his way back to the footpath, where he had been found by a search party.

'Thats it,' said Henry, and sat down in sudden exhaustion on the plumped-up cushions.

For once Mrs Pinkerton-Porke overlooked this faux pas. She looked across at the policeman who was folding away his notebook and avoiding her eyes. He harrumphed to himself and settled his helmet back on his head. Mrs Pinkerton-Porke promptly burst into tears. Her husband pulled her into the crook of his broad arm and patted her gently on the shoulder. The two men looked at each other and then at the sleepy boy on the settee.

'Now, now,' Mr Pinkerton-Porke soothed his wife, 'everything will be all right and tight, you'll see.' For it was plain to all the adults that her son was suffering from some sort of delusion or hallucination.

The inspector shook hands with them both and informed them that they would be sealing the opening of the mine securely to stop another potential tragedy. His advice was to take the lad to see the counselor once again, and casting them a pitying look he removed himself from the room, nearly falling over Percival who was crouching by the door.

He wondered as he left and called his squadron together, if the poor lad would ever recover.

Percival's blonde good looks turned green with envy. He was on his best behaviour and waited for a chance to get Henry on his own, but the boy clung to his mother like a limpet, and Percival found himself frustrated at every turn.

He was so angry with himself for letting that snotty little boy hog the limelight. I should have gone in there he thought to himself. I wouldn't have bothered with sodding sandwiches when there were jewels to collect from the walls!

The counselor made little headway with Henry, for he stuck resolutely to his tale. He appeared a normal boy in every other way, and eventually it was decided to let him get back to his schooling, and just see how he went on.

Percival bided his time. He appeared to be studying hard with excellent results for he knew who were the best students and bullied and threatened them into doing his schoolwork for him. He set himself to the task of worming his way into Mrs Pinkerton-Porke's heart and good books, so he became centre stage again. When no-one was around he set upon Henry, pinching and poking him, demanding as much information on the layout of the mine with its jeweled tunnels as he could.

Mrs Pinkerton-Porke spoiled him, overwhelmed by his handsome features and his acts of kindness as he assisted with chores round the house and helped her cope with 'this difficult time.' For once local people had heard Henry's story the Pinkerton-Porkes had become subject to gossip and pitying glances about 'that poor lad.'

With time the villagers found other things to gossip about and Mrs Pinkerton-Porke was able to hold her head high and look down her long nose at them as she had before. She could sniff with displeasure as she passed men drinking outside the local pub, and snub the pretentious well-wishers who tried to engage her in conversation.

One evening, dressed in all their finery, the Pinkerton-Porkes tucked Henry into bed, kissed their golden beamish boy goodnight and set off for an evening of musical entertainment in the city.

Percival waved them goodbye from the window, watching the Bentley swing majestically out of the driveway.

The Cuckoo Pit

Once they were out of sight he ran lightly downstairs, and listened at the maid's door. The gentle sound of snoring convinced him that she was already deeply asleep.

He let himself into his father's workshop and took a heavy torch, a bag, and a chisel, before grabbing his coat, and putting on his walking boots. He left by the back door, shutting it gently, pressing the latch back into place with a click. Then using the light from the torch, he made his way from the house, down to the foot path and towards the mineshaft opening.

Henry pulled the curtains closed again as he backed away from the window. He had woken at the sound of the door latch closing, and watched the gilded head of Percival disappear across the fields with just the swing of light from the torch visible. A small smile crossed his face, and he scrambled back into bed and drew up the bedclothes.

Percival stumbled on in the darkness, tripping over molehills and roots before reaching the mine shaft. Scrambling through brambles he played the light from the torch over the recently fixed metal sheeting and replaced razor wire.

He swore softly to himself. What had Henry said? He played the boy's story through his head and recollected the exit deep in the woods. He would have to use that. He scrambled up the bank and slipping and stumbling through the copse searched in the darkness for the exit tunnel. Falling over tree roots he fell down a small incline and then felt the ground open up beneath him and he was suddenly plummeting through a dark tunnel, the light from the torch bouncing crazily around as he fell until he landed with a hard bump on the tunnel floor.

He got to his feet and brushed down his breeches. He knew he had lost the chisel on the way down as he fell, and picking up the torch he flashed the light round the cavern he found himself in. There were no lanterns burning, and no evidence of tallow from burning candles.

It smelt musty and he could hear nothing but dripping water and the sound of the stream Henry had talked about. There were no glittering jewels caught in the light of the torch.

Percival pushed forward, torch in one hand, bag in the other, taking a path along one of the tunnels, feeling his way, using the light to scan every part of the walls. They dripped water and oozed black sooty mud, but no emeralds glittered and no diamonds sparkled.

He retraced his steps and set off down another tunnel. The oppressive weight of the rocks, the steady drip of water and the narrowing of the tunnel began to unnerve Percival. The light from the torch shone into the darkness and revealed only thick shadows and the remains of old timbers, originally used to support the roof of the cave.

He didn't want to admit it but he began to feel afraid, and the shadows edging the torch light seemed sinister and threatening. Retracing his steps he took another turning, and then panicking ran back, falling and bruising his knees. His skin began to itch and he became hotter and hotter.

Stopping, he removed his coat and dumped it on the floor. The itching became maddening and he flung open his shirt and scratched at his chest. He shone the torch on his skin and was horrified to see something growing out of his flesh and frightened, he scratched harder. They looked like quills of feathers sprouting from his chest and running along his arms. His back prickled all over and he leant against the wall and rubbed against the solid rock for some relief.

Suddenly Percival dropped the torch, unable to hold it any longer. It rolled and lay casting shadows from the light on the ground. The bag fell from his grasp. He looked at his hands. To his horror they were changing, the bones adapting into wings, and more feathers emerged. His chest expanded, now covered in feathers, and he stepped out of his boots to see his feet transformed into thin bones with claws. His arms fluttered at his side, and his trousers split and fell apart as a feathered tail developed.

Frantic, he turned and began to hop back the way he had come. He could feel his face changing, the bones altering and he sobbed in terror. His mouth pursed and pinched and grew slowly into a beak.

He fluttered along the floor, flapping his grey wings uselessly, until he reached the cavern. Blinking his pale blue rounded eyes he realised that he could not escape from the exit so far above him, hidden again by the mud and soil he had dislodged earlier. The hole was completely blocked and no moonlight shone through. The narrowness of the shaft walls with nothing to grip on to prevented him from climbing out. He fluttered his wings and flew madly at the wall of dirt and mud, futilely hitting it time and time again until exhausted, he tumbled back to the floor with a flutter of feathers.

Percival calmed slightly as the space became wider and less claustrophobic. He concluded that he would have to stay the night in this ghastly place and he hopped about the floor, waiting for the evening to pass.

He wanted to awaken from this nightmare and hear the sound of his rescuers calling for him.

He knew that as he was the favourite and brilliant son, a search party would be sent out as soon as the light dawned, and once the police found him he could get some medicine to sort out this dreadful feather problem.

Dawn came, with tiny threads of light spilling into the cave and as the day grew brighter and longer Percival heard the voices of his rescuers calling his name as they beat through the copse. He heard dogs barking and the whistles of the police.

He opened his beak and shouted, 'I'm here! In here! Save me!' but all that came out of his beak was 'Cuckoo! Cuckoo!' He flew with renewed vigour at the exit, but no one heard.

He called for a long time. 'Cuckoo! Cuckoo!' until the voices faded into the distance and the dark returned. Percival stopped shouting. He stretched his wings tiredly, blinking bright eyed in the dusky light. Hopping in the dirt, hungry and thirsty, he drank from the stream and found grubs to peck and eat. He would try again tomorrow.

And tomorrow.

And the next day.

And the next.

But they never did find the golden, lithesome, handsome young Percival.

Police and rescue workers searched for weeks on end, accompanied only by the cuckoo's call amid the birdsong, as they scrutinised the wooded areas, the beck and riverbank.

Posters were put up offering rewards for information, but no one came forward. The mine head was checked and found to be sealed and untampered with, and any exit that Henry had talked about in his incredible story was never found.

Weeks went by and the police scaled down their search, and finally left the case as open but inactive.

After a year Mr and Mrs Pinkerton-Porke, unable to bear the loss of their angel child and the constant gossiping of the locals, took their young son Henry with them and moved closer to London and aunt Valetta and the twins.

India and China remained with their aunt Valetta in London. Their aunt had taught them about fashion and design, and encouraged them to live up to their names. Consequently India dressed only in saris and China only in cheongsam dresses. They had become something of minor celebrities and 'It' girls. They dabbled in fashion and the arts and became reality TV stars and enjoyed every minute of it.

Henry settled into his new school and the story of the bejeweled mine was never mentioned again.

Henry had seen no reason to inform the police that Percival had woken him as he left the manor house that night. He had seen no reason to tell them how he had watched from his bedroom window the light from the torch tracking along the footpath to the old mine.

The villagers were glad to see the 'For Sale' sign at the manor house. To lose one son and then find him, poor lad, not quite right in the head with his incredible stories, and then to lose another boy! Well, there was something very strange there, they murmured darkly.

The manor house was sold to a large family with a variety of animals and dogs who spilled into the village community with enthusiasm and energy. The mother sent her children to the local school and they played with their friends and walked back home along the footpath by the stream and the copse.

Whispered stories of the lost boys were passed on and children ran past the mine entrance as quickly as they could before calming and shrieking with laughter as they splashed in the stream.

As they played, the children listened to hear the cuckoo calling loudly from somewhere, hidden deep in the woods, close to the sealed and abandoned old mine, and then ran home to tell their mother that they had heard the first cuckoo calling, and spring was here.

The End.

The Cuckoo Pit

LITTLE JENNY WREN

She had lain for so many years amongst the reeds and waters of the lake that her flesh had long since rotted and silt had covered her bones. The lake, long ago abandoned, had shrunk in size, so she rested in the last of the shallows. Bulrushes had grown through the locks of her hair, at first gently stirring her curls, and tiny fish darted through the weeds until they retreated along with the last of the water.

The bones of a small whippet, along with the decayed remains of rope tied loosely around its neck, lay nestled in her arms, as they had when they drowned together all those years ago.

At times, when the wind quivered through the reeds and the owls called in the woods, she and the dog stirred from their grave and climbed the dried lake banks, threading through the footpath, returning to the Tudor manor house nestled in the folds of the fields and woods.

She had watched her secret friend, the son of the manor house owner, grow to adulthood. They had met and played and fallen in love, and never told a soul about their friendship for she was of gypsy stock and he was gentry.

He had been distraught when she had first vanished, and had often sat on the bank of the lake, unaware of her there beside him. He had cried, fists in his eyes, wiping tears from his cheeks, for they had loved each other, and he assumed her family had taken her away. With no one to see him he threw bouncing stones across the lake, chasing memories, as he grew into a melancholic young man.

He had been killed in the Great War. Fleetingly they had been aware of each other as he died and fled the unspeakable horror of the trenches, but unable to hold to each other, they had touched briefly, before he was gone.

It had left her with a deep sadness, but still she had to wait, watching the seasons and the years change.

She saw the manor house empty as its fortunes changed. It became a farmhouse with tenants who changed every few years, outbuildings fell and rotted, and then finally the doors closed and the house, undisturbed except by the birds and wildlife, fell into decline.

Her delicate etherial hands felt the flowers as they grew each year, and the whippet's paws made no imprint on the grass as they played on the overgrown lawn in front of the leaded windows. The house, as abandoned now as the lake, sat still and silent on the land.

The Temple Elfold brooded in its surroundings, huge gothic wrought iron gates marking the entrance, overgrown with brambles and honeysuckle. Birds swooped and sang, the sun rose and sank, and time passed.

The house waited. The young girl with the whippet at her side made daisy chains and waited. She was lonely and tired of the waiting, but she knew the time would come when it would be over and they would all be free again.

* * *

Erin looked out of the window as Marcus slowed the car, and stopped at the end of the lane. The Ford Cortina had bumped down the rutted track towards the Temple Elfold, grounding occasionally and causing Marcus to curse under his breath. It was misty, and water droplets clung to the trees and shrouded everything in dampness and muffled the birds' calls.

Wild dog roses clung to their clothes as they climbed out of the car and approached the huge gates. Water soaked through their shoes, and damp beaded their hair. Erin's eyes widened and she laid a hand on the cold wrought iron and looked through at the house.

'Oh wow, how beautiful is that.' She looked across at her husband, and caught his grin.

He drew her into the crook of his arm and rested his chin on the top of her head.

'I knew you would love it.'

The house lay dreaming within a dream, shrouded in mist, its age and elegance blending into the overgrown trees, weeds and shrubs that enfolded it. It had been built in Tudor times, and added to over many centuries.

Its leaded windows and soft mellow bricks and elegant chimneys were markers of its age and social history. Aged terracotta tiles contrasted against the lower half of the building, and steps led to a magnificent oak door.

Marcus moved the 'For Sale' sign to one side and pulled the latch open on the gates. They creaked and moaned with protest as he wedged them open, dragging back the brambles so that they could both walk through.

'What do you think?'

His wife was staring entranced at the house. 'It's fabulous Marcus. I think I need to see inside.'

They walked up the overgrown drive which swept to the front door. Erin stepped over and around a few shrubs, half noting that at one time there had been a box hedge there, wiped the leaded window clear of water, and tried to peer inside.

'Well, it's just as well I have the key then isn't it?' and smiling, he pulled a huge metal key from deep within his coat pocket. 'Front door key.'

Erin laughed. 'That's some door key, but then it's some house!'

Marcus said, 'The agent didn't want to come out today, so he let me have the key so we could view it. I think he despairs of selling it.' He fitted the key in the massive lock and it opened as easily as if it had been oiled the day before. The huge wooden door gave way under the push of his hand.

'There is no electric. He says it still has the old gas lamps, so I brought a torch.'

Erin followed him in, her eyes adjusting to the change of light. It smelt old and musty, and at first glance cobwebs and rubbish on the floors distracted her. But then she looked again.

There were added extensions with nooks and crannies awaiting exploration. Darkened mouldering salon rooms closed for years, beckoned her to open the doors and let the light in. Once lit only by the now obsolete gas lights and heated by open fires, they still retained a dusty, faded beauty.

Two curving staircases with elegant balustrades led to the beautiful large bedrooms.

Her heels echoed on the wooden floors as they wandered through the house. The kitchen was out of a Dickens novel with its huge range, inglenook fireplace and bread oven.

'I know there is just about everything to do, but I think it's worth it. What do you think?' Marcus watched his wife's face. She had a smear of dirt on her cheek, and she had wandered hand in hand with him, spellbound.

'I think if you don't buy it we are going to head to the divorce courts.' And she giggled and wrapped her arms round him. 'Marcus it's absolutely wonderful! It wants us here I can feel it! How can it not be ours with a fabulous name like the Temple Elfold?'

'Spooky wife.' He said. Her obsession with spirits and ghosts was something that he loved, hated and found maddening about her. She often gave card readings to friends, and was a devout believer in a spiritual life. He had known her since childhood, and she had always been a fey creature, but it never stopped him loving her. She was the complete opposite of him, his feet so firmly on the ground sometimes he felt rooted there.

They entertained friends in their London house, with long intense dinner parties filled with music and dancing. They smoked weed, listened to The Beatles, Françoise Hardy, The Rolling Stones, and wore the latest fashions. Erin studied crystals and practiced yoga, and held workshops for life drawing and 'the goddess within.' He worked the stock markets and was very successful, although the hours were long and stressful.

Recently they had both begun to think about a different home and lifestyle. Somewhere to raise a family, reconnect with the countryside, and enjoy more time together. The particulars of the Temple Elfold had dropped through the letter box at exactly the right time.

He carefully locked the door and tested his weight against it just to make sure. They walked round the gardens and looked across to the fields and dried-out lake in the distance. Much as he enjoyed the view, Marcus was distracted by his wife's long legs and her mini skirt. Thank god for Mary Quant he thought to himself.

'The dogs will love it here as well,' Erin said dreamily. The sun had burnt off the last of the fog, and the view was breathtaking. She could imagine their two greyhounds running loose, and dear old Bear would be able to potter about to his heart's content. He had been with her as long as she could remember, her lovely lurcher with his grizzled face.

They walked back to the car, discussing plans and working out what offer to put forward. Marcus had received an inheritance from a great uncle, which put the house within their grasp. As the wrought iron gates closed behind them, Erin glanced up.

A young girl watched them from the bedroom window. Erin jumped. She could just see a whippet type dog at her side. As she stared up, the hairs on her arms rising, the girl lifted a hand in greeting and waved and then stroked the top of the dog's head. Erin drew in a sharp breath.

Marcus looked up, and then at his wife. 'What is it? What's wrong?'

'Nothing, nothing.' She said quickly. The house and its atmosphere were not threatening or dark other than being old and run down. She had imagined, as she moved from room to room, hearing a stately harpsichord playing music from centuries before.

The ghosts of the Templars moved through the gardens but did not disturb her. But the small girl had taken her by surprise. She looked again, but the girl had gone.

Best not to mention it to Marcus just at the moment as she knew he was completely sceptical of these things.

They got in the car, and reversing it carefully, turned and drove slowly back down the track.

The girl clapped her hands together and ran with the dog into the garden.

The waiting was over.

* * *

After that, it all happened very quickly. The Temple Elfold had been on the market for some time, and their offer of £16,000 secured it. The solicitors went to work, and several weeks later, at the beginning of summer, a selection of keys on a huge ring were handed to them and they were free to move in and begin the renovation of the historic manor.

They managed with candles and storm lanterns until the electric went in, and Erin learnt how to tackle the huge ancient Aga. With Marcus commuting to London during the week, it fell to Erin to organise the builders, plumbers, gas fitters and every other tradesman that was needed for what they discovered was a complete refurbishment.

Beautiful panelled walls were revealed hidden behind plywood fixtures and stud walls, and stately fireplaces long concealed, were restored to their former glory.

Mouldering drapery was replaced with vibrant Laura Ashley hand-made curtains, with matching cushions. The elegant chairs and tables piled up in the barns were hauled out, polished and mended and returned to the salon and dining rooms. Chandeliers re-appeared to sparkle and send rainbow patterns through the house.

Friends came down from London to help decorate, and then partied on the lawn into the early hours. The house came back to life. Flowers in vases appeared at the windows, the smell of cooking pervaded the rooms, and pots of jam and chutney began to fill the pantry. Chickens clucked outside as they roamed in their pen, and fresh eggs were collected daily.

The greyhounds loped through the grounds at high speed and then collapsed upside down wherever a suitable settee or bed could be found. Erin's lurcher Bear followed her wherever she went, or snored peacefully beside the Aga.

Erin saw the child with the whippet now and again. The greyhounds approached but were unsure how to play with a speedy, ghostly hound that vanished into thin air, and Bear just stared. The girl stood by the path to the lake, sometimes playing, but never coming back to the house.

If approached she ran back down the path before melting away. Sometimes Erin woke from a deep sleep convinced she had heard her name whispered, and if she looked out of the window she would catch a glimpse of what looked impossibly like water on the dried out lake.

She finally told Marcus about their ghost and as predicted he told her she was imagining things. When she tried to argue the point they both become angry, and had their first row in their new home. She could not understand how he could not see her.

'Maybe because she's not there' was the retort.

It had taken time for the dust to settle, and they had agreed to set this issue on one side.

Now, pouring over the endless bills collecting on the delicate antique writing desk rescued from the local junk shop, Marcus ran his fingers through his hair and pushed his chair back.

'I don't know about the Temple Elfold,' he remarked to Erin, 'I think I will have to re-christen it the Money Pit.'

Erin put her arms round his shoulders and snuggled in to his neck, breathing in his scent. She loved him so much. 'I love you,' she said, pressing kisses into his throat.

Marcus laid down his pen and set the bills to one side. 'Are you doing anything this afternoon?' he asked.

'No, just sorting out the herb garden.'

Marcus entwined his wife's fingers with his. He drew her forward and kissed her lips. ' I think the herbs can wait.' And smiling the two of them headed up the stairs. Bear lifted his white head where he lay by the range and watched for a minute then lay down again with a sigh.

Erin and Marcus lay wrapped round each other, the late afternoon light spilling across the bedroom floor. Lovemaking had left them both replete, tangled in the bed sheets, utterly content.

Erin trickled her fingertips across Marcus' chest and edged closer. 'Marcus.' He grunted a little, nearly asleep.

'Marcus, do you remember that young girl I told you about?'

His eyes opened, and she felt his muscles tense beneath her hand. 'What about her?'

Erin drew a deep breath. 'I want to ask the local vicar to come down here and bless our home. I want to ask him if there is a history of a girl dying here.'

'Jesus Christ, Erin!' Marcus threw back the bedclothes and leapt out of the bed. He turned to look at her, all sleek woman and blonde tumbled hair. 'Why are you doing this? Why are you doing this now?' he was suddenly furious with her, and turned, grabbing his clothes and pulling them on.

She sat up. 'Marcus -'

'No, Erin. No. I spend all my time working to get the money for this damn place you wanted so much, and I just don't need this, not now, not ever.'

He could hear himself shouting, livid, all the frustrations of work, money and endless commuting suddenly centred on her. 'I don't want to hear that you think there are ghosts here, because we are not moving again. Sometimes I think - ' and managed to stop himself.

She stared, flinty eyed at him 'You think what, Marcus? You wanted this house too, so don't just blame me. What is it you think Marcus? That I'm mad? That you would be happier if you hadn't married me? What is it you think?' and she stood up clutching the sheet. 'I'm not mad. She is here. It's not my fault you've got the sensitivity of a boiled egg!'

They both stared at each other. For a second Marcus was tempted to laugh, but he wanted to be angry, to blame her for everything, so 'Great. Bloody great.' he said bitterly, and slammed out of the bedroom.

He ran quickly down the stairs, and the two greyhounds leapt to their feet and followed him as he strode out into the garden. He whistled to them and walked across the lawn, taking the path to the lake. As he walked, he calmed down. The greyhounds ran about pouncing on mice in the long grass, their joie de vivre easing his foul mood.

At the edge of the lake he stopped and frowned as he thought over the row with his spooky wife. He sighed and put it out of his mind.

There was nothing to be done now. He just wished that she would stop this thing about the child.

He sat down and watched a grasshopper climbing a blade of grass before it disappeared with a tremendous spring. He could hear the shrill calls of swifts above him and the skylarks singing, hovering high in the sky. Butterflies fluttered, looking for a place to settle, displaced by the dogs running through the grass. He pulled out a blade of grass and chewed on it. The lake was a fair size, and as he sat brooding, an idea formed in his head.

Getting up, he walked the perimeter. If it was cleared and re stocked and filled, it would make a good sized lake, and if they sold fishing permits they could make some money, maybe even do bed and breakfast. He scrambled down the side bank, to estimate its depth, and found a few inches of water soaking his feet. It would need digging out he mused.

His head full of plans, he continued on his walk.

At the Temple Elfold, his wife clicked her fingers at Bear and loaded him with difficulty into the backseat of her mini.

She drove off without a backward glance, still seething. She wanted a few hours to herself, away from the constant demands of the house renovation, bills, and her husband's disbelief. Perhaps a walk by the sea would calm her.

Bear laid his head over the front seat and put his long pointed nose out of the window as they drove away, wise enough to know that a coastal walk was on the cards.

That evening the atmosphere was still frosty. Finally Marcus went in search of his wife in the kitchen where he could hear her banging pots about.

'Look,' he said. 'I'm sorry, OK?'

She cut him a glance and ignored him.

'I am trying to apologise. You know I don't believe in all that stuff.'

'I know you don't Marcus, but I do. You've always known how I feel about this kind of thing.' She looked at him, noticing the shadows under his eyes from working so much overtime. He had lost weight as well she realised.

The house had taken a toll on him, thank God it was nearly finished. 'I know the house has used up nearly all our money, and I know how hard you work.' She wiped her hands on the tea towel and lent back on the pine table.

'Erin, I don't believe in ghosts. I don't feel anything here other than it's our home. A happy one if we can make it that way. I want to have our kids here. I don't want to hear about dead little girls haunting the place.'

Her lips tightened. Erin looked at her husband. How to get round this she wondered. Could she pretend that she saw nothing? She fiddled with her wedding ring. In her head she heard her mother's voice 'what you don't know doesn't hurt you.' She could sort this out herself, not involve Marcus. The vicar wouldn't mention it if she asked him not to. 'OK' she said.

'That's it? OK?'

'Yep.'

Marcus felt huge relief, and a slightly uneasy feeling that he had missed something. He started laying the table, and said, 'While I was at the lake this afternoon, I had a really good idea,' and he began to put forward the plans to dredge the lake, refill and restock it.

The Cuckoo Pit

His enthusiasm was so patent that Erin forgot their row, and heads together they worked out where the trees could be planted, and where the platforms for the anglers could be installed. They had plenty of space for bed and breakfast guests.

The house wrapped itself around them like an old blanket, warm and comforting, and at the lake the girl smiled and lay down beside the dog, stroking its face.

* * *

Marcus had to get a large digger in to shift the silt and clogged weeds from the lake bed. He had taken a weeks holiday to organise it, and strode down to the lake when the machine arrived with the foreman and an assistant.

It was a feat in itself getting the digger to the lake, and then they set to with the JCB digging in and emptying its load out on the areas required for a viewing platform. They worked steadily for an hour or so until the assistant shouted and held up his hand to stop the spill of earth from the machine.

Marcus could see him looking at something in the soil mixture, and then he was shouting and beckoning to Marcus, and the machine's roar shut down, and there was blessed silence for a moment. Marcus made his way to the foreman. 'What is it?'

'Bones, sir, we've got bones.' And he indicated the heap of soil spilled onto the meadow. Marcus swallowed, and bent over the soil spill. He could see protruding from the earth small bones, perhaps ribs, and then as he bent closer, a small human skull could be seen half buried in the soil.

Marcus staggered slightly, and his hand clutched at the cold metal of the machine. He felt disorientated, sounds echoed in his ears, and for a terrible moment he thought he was going to pass out. He could see the foreman saying something, but he couldn't hear him.

His gaze fixed on that small skull and he wanted to weep. He was aware of the vague whisper of his name and strangely, for a moment, he had an image of a wide smile and laughing hazel eyes flash through his mind. As he stared at the bones he knew instinctively it was the girl Erin had seen.

His clutching hand slipped on the edge of the digger, and a small flint cut into his hand and brought him back to awareness. The foreman was looking at him with some concern.

'You all right sir?'

Marcus stood up and tried to gather himself together. 'Yes, I wasn't expecting anything like this.'

'Bit of a shock to me as well! You'll need to get the police out,' he called up to the machine operator. 'All right Bill, we need to just leave everything as it is until the police get here.'

'I'll go to the house and call the police.' Marcus glanced back at the soil. 'If you could both come with me as they may need to speak to you.' He pulled his jumper off over his head and very carefully laid it over the visible bones. 'Erin will make you a cup of tea while we wait.'

Together they walked back to the house, removing their muddy boots before entering the kitchen. Bear wagged his tail.

Marcus called to his wife 'Erin! Erin!' She appeared at the top of the stairs, startled by the note in his voice.

'What is it?'

He was dialing 999 on the phone. He looked up, and she was shocked at the expression on his face. 'I'm calling the police. We found what looks like human remains in the lake. I would be really grateful if you could make tea for us all.' And he turned back to the phone as it was answered. 'Police,' he said.

The police arrived and interviewed them all, while a forensics team went to the lake and gradually collected and removed all the bones. The detective and constable left the house and conferred with their colleagues as they stood by the digger.

The inspector returned and accepted a cup of tea. 'Well, we believe that these are bones that have been there for quite some time due to the decomposition so they are known as ancient bones. We have collected all the evidence and our lab will be examining them and then we will contact you with the outcome. I will check historical records for any missing persons, as much as we can in terms of the age of these bones. I would ask that you cease any digging until we have further results.'

Marcus paid the men to remove the digger until a more suitable time. The light had gone by the time everyone had left and the couple were on their own again.

Despite the warmth of the day, Marcus was shivering slightly, so Erin quietly set about building a fire and presented him with a glass of whisky. She curled up beside him as he sat, absorbing the heat from the fire.

He said suddenly ' I could see her skull Erin, she can't have been much more than a child.' and as if something had cracked inside of him, he let out a sob and clutched her so tightly that it hurt. She held him, just held him. After a while he looked up at her. 'I don't know why I feel like this. I feel as if I knew her. How can I feel that when all that is left is her bones?'

Erin said nothing, pressing small kisses into his hair. She whispered 'It's going to be all right. You found her, it is what she wanted. Maybe she can be at peace now.'

He sat a little straighter and took a deep drink of whisky, letting it burn through him. 'The police will let us know as soon as they can, I suppose.'

They sat as the darkness drew in all around them, comforting each other in silence, lit by firelight. The dogs came through to join them, laying in contented heaps on the rugs as they stared into the flames.

It took a few weeks for the forensic results and investigation to complete. When the call came that the inspector wanted to discuss the case with them, Marcus took the day off and they drove to the police station together for their appointment.

The inspector shook hands with them both and settled them into seats.

'Well, we have concluded our investigations. We believe the bones are of young woman, aged between ten and fourteen years of age.

The coroner tells us that they have been in the lake for approximately seventy years, possibly longer, but its hard to be more precise. We found small fragments of leather from the soles of her shoes, but little else that survived the water. We also found the remains of a small dog with her. There are no indications of violence on the bones.

Our investigations reveal no missing persons recorded in a twenty year period from 1890 to 1910 from local paper reports or archives. These would be the approximate decades to match the bones.

There are also no murder enquiries at that time, and this child was not recorded as missing. We have no further information to account for her death.'

He shuffled some papers. ' It is possible that this was some sort of accident, perhaps she went into the lake with the dog and couldn't get out, but this is merely speculation. Sadly we may never know why she died, or who she is.'

They discussed the possibilities for a while, and the inspector agreed that the bones could be released for a cremation which the local authority would pay for, as the deceased was no relation to them. Erin and Marcus would collect the ashes and find a suitable resting place for them.

They left the station and drove back to the house. Marcus stood for a while, looking through the gates at the Temple Elfold as he had that first time.

Erin took his hand. 'Do you regret it?' she asked him. He looked down at their hands clasped together, and smiled. His face was relaxed and his eyes were peaceful. 'No. Not for a minute. This is our home, with all its history, good and bad. Time to make our mark on it.'

They opened the gates and went through to the historic manor house, beautiful in the setting sun with flowers of every colour rioting in the borders. Shrubs and trees gracefully encircled the manor and an emerald lawn with its gate and path led onwards to the lake. They unlocked the magnificent door and went inside.

Erin ran upstairs and changed her clothes for slacks and plimsolls. As she glanced out of the window she saw the girl, wraithlike, standing on the opposite side of the wrought iron gates, her face turned upwards. Erin walked slowly to the window and looked down. The girl looked up, and smiled and nodded slightly. She lifted a hand in greeting, and Erin lifted her own hand in acknowledgement. The girl turned down the lane, took a few paces, and melted away.

Erin never saw her again.

Life returned to normal for Marcus and Erin. They completed the renovation of the lake, and recreational fishermen arrived at weekends.

Anglers sat for hours on the bank close to the glittering water, waiting for the fish to bite, and then in the evenings came back to the house to eat hearty meals and talk about the one that got away.

One night, returning home through a wild and windy end of summer storm, Marcus shouted for Erin as he came through the door.

He had a bundle wrapped in his coat, which he placed carefully in her arms as she ran to him.

'I nearly ran her over. She was lying in the lane. She is in a dreadful state. I'm not sure she will survive.' and he gently peeled the material back to reveal an emaciated little lurcher, shivering in terror, hidden in the folds of his coat.

Erin clutched the dog to her and went through to the kitchen. 'Move over, Bear.' She laid the small dog close to the Aga, where the heat would warm her and wrapped a towel round her until only her head was showing. 'Marcus can you get a bowl of dog food?'

They watched as the little dog ravenously ate the food and licked the bowl clean. Bear stood wagging his tail proudly and the two greyhounds looked in, inspected the new arrival, then went back to the settee and the warmth of the fire. Erin looked up at Marcus.

'I think she's a fighter. I think she is going to be all right.' She ran a hand down the dog's back, feeling her spine sticking out. 'She's a little whippet type I think.' The little dog quivered and shook with nerves, and Marcus bent over and stroked the dog's head.

'You'll have to think of a name for her if we are going to keep her.'

Erin looked up.

'Of course we are keeping her! I shall call her Little Jenny Wren.' The dog sighed and curled into the warm towel and shut her eyes.

Marcus raised his brows. 'That was quick! Little Jenny Wren. Yes, I like that. Little Jenny Wren it is.'

Erin smiled and reached up to hug her husband. Bear woofed at them. They laughed and began to talk about the day and Erin sorted out a meal for them both. Sitting at the pine table, eating together, they watched Bear settle his old frame back on his bed next to Little Jenny Wren.

Marcus felt his muscles relax and the long day slide away. His wife's face, radiant with beauty in the soft lights, caught at his heart and he reached forward to kiss her. It had been a tough year, but he felt at peace with everything that had happened.

The Temple Elfold glowed in the night from its new electric lighting, and restored splendour. The rain started as the wind died, and droplets of water shone like jewels on the windows.

The water in the lake reflected the moonlight, and Little Jenny Wren stretched out her poor emaciated body, relaxing from the warmth of the Aga. She opened her soft, dark brown eyes and watched her new owners chatting and laughing over their meal. She was home.

The End.

ABOUT THE AUTHOR:

Jo Brodie lives and works in West Sussex. She is an artist and writes and illustrates her own short stories which can be found on Amazon. She supports a variety of Greyhound and Lurcher rescue groups, the PDSA, and charities that she has a personal interest in.

Her life changed upon the introduction of a lurcher puppy called Mr Fred, in ways that she could not believe, and led to many more lurchers joining the family over the years. Known affectionately as the Zoo Gang, these hounds have passed away, but other rescue hounds have arrived to keep her walking along the coastal paths, and to inspire her paintings and stories.

Her paintings can be found on her Etsy shop
https://www.etsy.com/uk/shop/jobrodieart

Short stories available as paperback or ebooks at
https://www.amazon.co.uk

The Dog Tails
The Star Dancer
The Singing Gates

Hounded! (poems)

Printed in Great Britain
by Amazon